CARAVAN

by Lawrence McKay, Jr.

illustrated by Darryl Ligasan

LEE & LOW BOOKS Inc. • *New York*

Manufactured in China by South China Printing Co., August 2014

Book design by Christy Hale
Book production by The Kids at Our House

The text is set in Weiss
The illustrations are rendered in acrylic on canvas. Gel mediums,
sandpaper, and pumice were used to achieve surface texture.
Some of the illustrations were inspired by the photographs of Roland and Sabrina Michaud
from their book, *Caravans to Tartary*, originally published in 1977 by Sté Nlle des Editions
du Chene, Paris, and reprinted by Thames & Hudson Inc., New York.

10 9 8 7 6 5 4 3 2
FIRST EDITION

Library of Congress Cataloging-in-Publication Data
McKay, Lawrence.
Caravan / by Lawrence McKay, Jr. ; illustrated by Darryl Ligasan. — 1st ed.
p.   cm.
Summary: A ten-year-old boy accompanies his father for the first time
on a caravan trip through the mountains of Afghanistan to the city
below to trade their goods at market.
ISBN 978-1-60060-346-4 (paperback)
[1. Caravans—Fiction. 2. Barter—Fiction. 3. Fathers and sons—Fiction.
4. Afghanistan—Fiction.] I. Ligasan, Darryl, ill. II Title.
PZ7.M4786575Car 1995
[Fic]—dc20   95-2037   CIP AC

afghanistan.

For Mother and Dad—L.M.

To my parents:
To my dad for showing me the world,
and to my mom for always giving me a home to come home to.
—D.L.

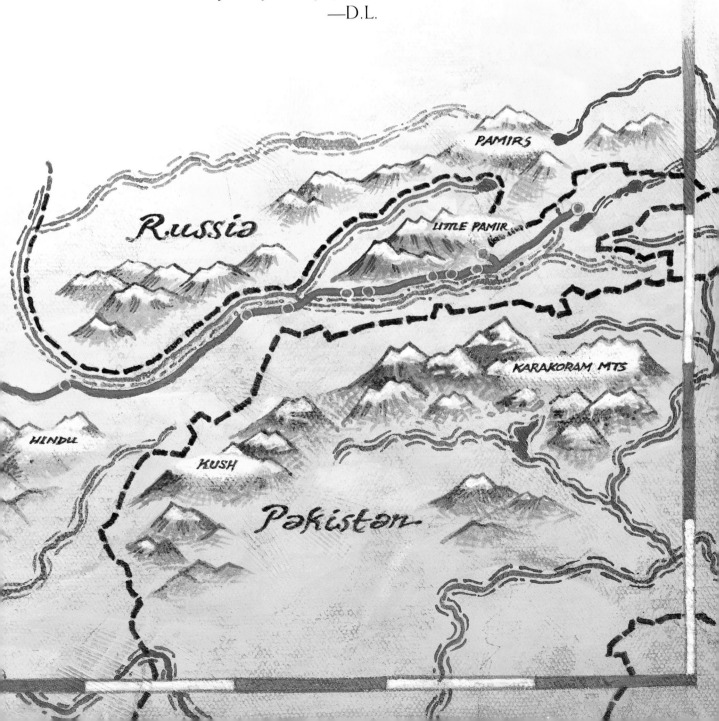

MY NAME IS JURA and I am ten years old.
Today I go on the caravan for the first time.
I carry my saddle and bedding to my mare,
waiting in the pasture under the hills.
My little sisters skip along beside me,
for it is the day I become a man,
and ride beside my father,
over the passes and through the snow,
in the caravan swaying back and forth,
where the mountains meet the sky,
and the trail leads ever on.

I am entrusted with three camels.
I drape layers of felt over their backs.
Their wooly fur is soft to the touch,
and their manes bristle under my fingers.
I lash heavy packs to their humps,
and then bring them up with sharp commands.

The packs are filled with furs and felts,
we'll trade for grain in the city.
My father is the leader of our caravan.
He knows the route and the way.
He climbs into his saddle and takes the reins,
then gives the word to depart.

As the drivers move their camels out,
I mount my mare and urge her forward.
I hope someday I'll be like my father,
guiding the camels through the Pamirs.
The camels are tied to each other.
Snowdrifts collapse in their wake.

We climb into the cold blue light,
toward sheer fields of snow and ice.
My breath is a white cloud,
and frost clutches my eyebrows.
A river rolls down the canyon,
roaring like a great winged dragon.

We pass the night inside a cave.
Dinner bubbles in a pot over the fire.
As the drivers sit talking in whispers,
I drop the cheese into the pot and stir.

Ripping a piece of bread in two,
I dip it in the melted cheese and eat.
My father pours tea from the chogun,
and I move nearer the reddening coals.

Mountains are giants hovering over us.
They must be spirits guarding the pass.
Sheets of snow whirl like howling ghosts,
and the sky ripples with lightning.
Leading my camels upward over the pass,
I ride single file behind my father.

I hear rockfalls clattering down cliffs,
and feel the trembling of an avalanche.
I talk my mare down the steep track.
My camels shamble along behind me.
As I pick my way over rocks and snow,
I grip the reins firmly in one hand.

I am careful not to slip on the ice
that shimmers with my reflection.
I gaze down the long winding valley,
and watch a boulder roll out of sight.
Wind opens a breach in the clouds.
From peaks ice glints in sunlight.

We trek along the meandering river,
watching rushes sway in the breeze.
Smelling the aroma of dates in the air,
I direct my camels up over a rise.
Below me the city unfolds,
like a carpet with mysterious designs.

Across the river the market is bustling.
The camels file over the bridge,
hooves clanking on the wooden boards.
I ride into our camp,
and dismount next to my father.
I light the fire and unpack our utensils.

As coals redden in the hearth,
I listen to the clamor of the town.
Remembering the silence of the snowy hills,
I dream of running through our pastures.
My eyelids are heavy, my head droops,
and I fall asleep against my saddle.

Dawn illuminates the cupolas of a mosque.
The townspeople jostle and gather around us.
Today we trade our skins and felts for grain,
and tomorrow we journey home.
My father sits down upon a kilim,
and rubs the grain between his fingers.
His eyes are steady, his voice unwavering,
and soon he strikes a fine bargain.

I stride through the city with my father.
From their stalls, merchants call out to us to buy.
We enter the portal to the covered bazaar,
where fragrances of spices linger in the air.
From a corner I watch as hanks of wool
are dyed with color then hung to dry.
The wool will be used to make kilims,
that will be sold across the world.

I kneel upon a carpet in the tea house.
The owner prepares a tray with cups.
He pours hot water from a samovar,
and I listen to my father laughing.
His eyes twinkle and his smile flashes,
as he talks about his trading.
I hold my cup in the bowl of my hands,
and listen as the men share their stories.

The caravan pulls away from the city,
past prayer flags and stone monuments.
Fog hangs over the valley like a tattered blanket,
and I lean close to my mare, hugging her.
I can feel the sudden chill frosting the air,
as we wend our way into the uplands.
Behind me the city fades in the mists,
and I huddle down into my coat,
in the caravan swaying back and forth,
where the mountains meet the sky,
and the trail leads ever on.

Inside a yurt I lie among a circle of men.
The walls flap back and forth in the wind.
My feet are pointed to the fire,
my bedding wrapped around me.
The fire flickers and spits,
and thoughts spiral upward in smoke.
As whispers are replaced by snores,
I close my eyes and drift off to sleep.

Camels curl around a bend in the river.
I hear rapids frothing under crusts of ice.
Snowflakes settle upon my shoulders,
and I brush the snow from my mare's ears.

Yearning to be running free in her pasture,
my mare's gait lengthens under me.
My body is weary, but my heart is singing,
as I listen to her hooves carrying me home.

I pull my camels into my family's winter camp.
My mother and sisters step from the doorway.
They wrap their arms around me,
wanting to know all about my journey.
We help my father unstrap the packs,
and carry the grain to the storehouse,

under the shadows of the snowy hills.
I take a deep breath of the mountain air,
and give thanks that I have returned,
from the caravan swaying back and forth,
where the mountains meet the sky,
and the trail leads ever on.

Author's Note

This story is based on the experiences of the Kirghiz caravaneers of Afghanistan. The Kirghiz are a nomadic people of Turko-Mongolian descent and are also indigenous to parts of Russia and China. In the Afghan Pamirs of the Hindu Kush Mountains, the Kirghiz caravans ply their trade routes. The Pamirs are a rugged land and span southern Russia, northeastern Afghanistan, and northern Pakistan. Here the term, "Roof of the World" was coined, for this area of grand mountain ranges—the Hindu Kush, the Karakoram, and the Himalaya—was once believed to be the highest land mass on earth.

Twice each winter, the Kirghiz caravaneers travel west for 10 days from the mountains to the regional capital. Here, they trade their felts and furs for grain. It is a journey of 125 miles over mountain passes, frozen rivers, and great valleys. Each driver brings his own horse and is responsible for three camels. Camels are the most valuable animals the caravaneers own: more valuable than yaks or horses or sheep. Camels are often associated with the desert, but these Bactrian "two-humped" camels are well acclimated to the high regions of the Central Asian Plateau. Able to carry up to 600 pounds and weighing up to half a ton, the camels are slow, but sure-footed.

Some of the words mentioned in the story may not be familiar to many readers. A *chogun* is a small teapot, while a *samovar* is a large metal container used to heat water for tea. *Mosques* are Muslim places of public worship; the rounded domes at the tops of mosques are called *cupolas*. A *kilim* is an Afghan carpet of tight woven design. Finally, a *yurt* is a circular tent made of thick felt with a small opening at the top to let out smoke from a low campfire that is kept burning inside. The caravaneers sleep in a star pattern, with their feet toward the fire, for warmth.